Remember Us with Smiles

By Grace and Gary Jansen

Illustrated by Barbara Bongini

LOYOLAPRESS.

For Edward and Charles,

Smile, laugh, sing, and dance, and always remember
to look for the beauty in life.

LOYOLAPRESS.

www.loyolapress.com
Chicago

© 2022 Loyola Press
Text © 2022 Grace & Gary Jansen
Illustrations Barbara Bongini
All rights reserved.

ISBN: 978-0-8294-5372-0
Library of Congress Control Number: 2021950046

Printed in the USA
22 23 24 25 26 27 28 29 30 31 CGC 10 9 8 7 6 5 4 3 2 1

Do you remember...

Do you remember the time we went to the park,
and we sat on the bench by that old elm tree,

and the sky was the color of honey?

Do you remember...

...that blustery autumn day when we walked in the overgrown field, and we were knights fighting a dragon?

6

We called it a dragon,

but it was really a bird.

Do you remember...

9

...how we read to you every night
before you went to sleep?

And do you remember when we piled up
your books to see if they were

taller

than

you?

You're taller now.
        Much, much **taller**.

Do you remember when you thought
there was a ghost in our room...

...and we scared it away?
And do you remember what you said?

Do you remember...

...when it would rain,
   and we would make a fort in the living room?

Just so you know,
you'll never be too big to build a fort.

Do you remember...

...all those times you got sick,
and I held you in my arms
until you felt better?

And the one time you had a bad fever?
When you fell asleep, I listened to you breathe,
right up until morning.

Do you remember when we used to lie
on the floor and draw pictures with crayons?

Or the time that skunk chased us during mini golf?

Pee-ew!

Do you remember the time we drove
in the snow to get ice cream?

Or the walks we took
in the dark-blue evenings
to look at the moon?

23

You know, someday you might forget some of these things. That's okay.

You see, it happens when you get older.

Sometimes you get, well, busy.

So if you do—
    if you forget the little things…

like all the movies we watched, all the pizza we ate, or all the songs we sang...

...or the day trips we took, or the towers we built, or the backyard baseball...even if you forget all that, I'm hoping that no matter where you go, no matter what you do, you remember us with smiles.

Because that is how we will
always remember you.